Prince Valiant's

PERILOUS VOYAGE

By HAROLD FOSTER

Text adapted by MAX TRELL
from the original story.

HASTINGS HOUSE

Publishers   *New York*

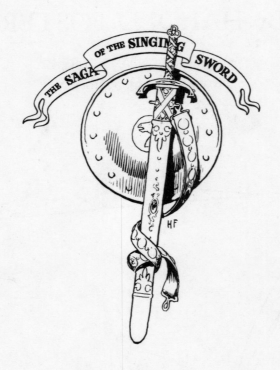

THE SAGA OF THE SINGING SWORD

THE PRINCE VALIANT SERIES

For a long while Queen Aleta watched the boat going away. It had a single sail, tall and full-spread; and in the stern, handling the long-hafted rudder, sat a solitary figure, dark of hair and stripped to the waist. Aleta kept her eyes fixed immovably on the figure, her lips half parted as if ready to speak aloud to him. But Val (for it was he) neither looked back nor so much as permitted himself to face in her direction when the boat came about, as it did more than once during the next half hour, to catch the frivolous, fragrant capfuls of breeze dancing out of the east.

And so at last the sail became a tiny speck in the immensity of the Aegean Sea. Then Aleta lay face down in the grass and her shoulders shook. But whether she laughed, or whether she cried, who could tell? She was young and beautiful and Queen of the Misty Isles. Why should she weep?

No, Val did not permit himself to look back. Over and over again he told himself that Aleta, for all her outward beauty, was the evil queen of an isle of evil. Had she not caused his crew to be murdered? He did not realize then that his crew had deserved their fate. There was no one to tell him the truth.

*As Prince Valiant glided into the harbor he saw
vessels from all quarters of the known world.*

Prince Valiant steered his boat idly and brooded, not caring overmuch
which way the winds blew him so long only as they blew him away from
Aleta of the golden hair . . . Aleta of the shattered dream . . . Aleta the
beautiful and the accursed.

But the miracle of youth is the miracle of sunrise. For out of the blackness and despair of night bursts the glory of another day. That is to say it
was not long before Val the Brokenhearted became once again Val the
High Hearted, singing to the gulls, laughing with the porpoises, racing his
boat against the shadows of the clouds as they went skimming across the
purple water. Almost without knowing he was doing so he began following
in the tracks of merchant vessels which appeared in increasing numbers as
the hours went by until finally Val found himself sailing into Piraeus, the
harbor of Athens.

Even now, centuries after its conquest by mighty Rome, Athens still
remained the city of elegance, of art, of culture, of learning; and Rome itself, conqueror though it was, humbly recognized this supremacy. Nor did
Athens turn its back on trade. As Prince Valiant glided into the harbor he
saw vessels from all quarters of the known world. And this was exactly to
his liking. For it was his hope to find one among all these ships which, heading northward, would set him once more on the beloved shores of his Britain. How long had he wandered? Three years. Three years of fighting, of

4

learning, of laughing and sorrowing. And perhaps, because the sorrowing had come last, it seemed the most.

Again the old sad mood was upon him. Aleta was going to be harder to forget than he thought. He would have to make a determined effort. What was it about love that made it defy all the laws of science and the universe? Aleta was miles away and yet . . . she was here. It was days since he last saw her face and yet . . . her eyes and her lips were before him.

Val scowled. He had other things to think of. The important immediate problem was to find a ship going to Britain.

He was by this time steering past the castlelike breakwater into the quiet inner mole. The harbor city of Piraeus lay spread out around him. And standing up in his boat and looking eastward he could see Athens lying just beyond.

There was Mount Pentelicus, famous for its quarries; and Mount Hymettus whose bees feasting on the flowered slopes made honey fit for the gods. Val fancied he could glimpse the Areopagus, dedicated to the war god Mars but where St. Paul once preached the gospel of the Prince of Peace.

And crowning all, Val thought he could clearly discern the Acropolis, that shimmering cluster of enchanted marble as warm and as vibrant as— Val paused then smiled as he admitted—as Aleta herself.

The Viking could scarcely keep his hands from hugging Val.

Having tied up his boat, Val mounted the stone steps leading to the water-front road.

The figure that met his eyes at the top of the steps he first mistook for a statue of Hercules or of one of the Olympian gods. But this was no statue. It was a living man, fully six feet tall, and brawny as an ox.

The man was a Viking. And this, of all things, was most remarkable. For even in a port as cosmopolitan as Piraeus a Viking was no common sight. By any reckoning this Viking's home could not be much less than three thousand miles away.

For a moment Val studied him. The northern face, weathered and bearded, wore an expression of anger. Then Val strode up and greeted him.

The Viking's jaw dropped. His eyes opened like saucers. Then—"Ho!" he roared, his face lighting up with the surprise and unexpected pleasure of hearing someone speaking his own tongue. He could scarcely keep his hands from hugging Val. "What wonder is this! You wear the outlandish garb of a Greek, and yet you speak the civilized language of a Viking!"

Val explained that the Viking tongue was native to his ear. "I was born in Thule—"

"Ho!" roared the Viking again. "Thule! Land of Winter! Land of Gale and Blizzard where a man breathes courage with every breath. Not this soft land of Greece where the sun makes you blink and yawn, and fries your brain and makes you so tenderhearted that every scoundrel who comes along may cheat you of your last crumb of bread or the last hair in your beard."

"Who has cheated you?" Val asked, realizing that this must account for the wrathful expression he had already noticed on the Viking's face. But the great bearded seafarer would say nothing more about this matter unless Val did him the honor of joining him in a wine shop.

"Nay," said Val. "I thank you kindly but my thoughts today are not on wine. Perhaps we shall meet again. In the meantime, happy voyage." As he said this Val turned to go. The Viking was not one easily dismissed.

Seizing Val he dragged him by force down the street. "You seem lonely, my boy," he said. "A drop or two of Grecian grape will do you no harm."

Val gave up the unequal struggle. To fight this hospitable giant one would need a fair-sized army.

Seated in the wine shop the Viking told his story. "I am Boltar, a respectable pirate and honest merchant. But I cannot do a profitable business with these wily Greeks. Hearken to me! I came here with a rich cargo of furs—no matter how I got them in the first place—and I thought to sell them for a good price. But these smart, shrewd, nimble-witted Greeks did me out of everything." The more indignant Boltar became the more he drank and the more he drank, the louder became his indignation. Val marvelled at his capacity for both—then suddenly toward dawn Boltar slid to the stone floor and slept. When at last he awoke, his head ached and he groaned. He insisted that only the feel of a deck under his feet and a vast ocean around him could cure him. Val knew better than to quarrel with him. Instead he accompanied him to the wharf where the Viking ship was moored.

Boltar's ship was a sorry sight . . . for his crew of Vikings were warriors all, who could eat like horses, drink like fish, fight like demons and die like heroes. At this particular moment they were heaped together in the bottom of the vessel like a catch of dead herring.

Boltar's thunderous roar brought them scrambling to their feet. "Awake you sodden rascals! Prepare to sail! Fetch the cargo! Up! Up!"

Val stared with amazement at the bales of silk and dyestuffs, the rugs, the jars of scented oils, the spices, the ornaments of gold and silver being stowed aboard the Viking craft. The crew brought these items to light from hidden places along the wharf.

"For someone who was cheated out of everything by the wily Greeks, you seem to have done pretty well," Val remarked to Boltar.

"Ah, my boy, you suspect our honesty. These are just some trifles we picked up here and there. We kept them hidden to prevent their being stolen from us. Don't tell me you think we are dishonest!" And Boltar grinned.

On discovering that Boltar's course lay to the west in the Inland Sea and north and that the ship would be touching the shores of Britain within a few weeks (the gods of the winds and storms willing), Val asked to be given passage. Boltar at once gave his consent.

Pirate or no, thought Val, this Viking offered the only ready means of getting back to far-off Britain. To make the journey overland might take a year or more, and was fraught with perils. And for a thief Boltar was comparatively honest, being direct and forthright rather than sly.

For many days the wind blew out of the east and the Viking ship scudded before it, passing islands innumerable, with the great continent of Africa lying always to the south. They coasted close to Sicily and Sardinia, stopping occasionally to replenish their supplies of meat, meal, honey, wine and fruit, for all of which Boltar paid generously, so that the villagers rejoiced. But occasionally, too, they did "business" with passing merchant

9

ships and likewise laid in supplies. But from them there were only complaints. And once, because his sea rovers needed exercise, Boltar sacked a fortified town on the North African shore. And so day by day they drew nearer to the ocean. Then came the morning when Val heard the Vikings shouting with joy and he beheld the towering Pillars of Hercules—Gibraltar one of them was later to be called—guarding blue Mediterranean from gray Atlantic. Val saw another sight as well, a battered, drifting ship. Val and Boltar boarded her. They found captain and crew stricken with fever

and dying of hunger. They gave them prompt aid . . . and out of this grew a strange adventure. For the captain thankfully gave them a great handful of golden nuggets and a crude map and said: "Here is gold, and here is a map which will show you where you may find more. But beware our fate."

Sending the unfortunate captain on his way, Boltar now turned to his own crew. "Our homes lie north. Gold lies south. Which way shall we sail?"

And with one voice the crew answered: "Southward for gold!"

Had the choice been his Val would have chosen otherwise. What gold

11

is as precious as the sight of home? But the choice was not his, and night after night he watched the North Star as it dipped ever lower on the horizon and knew they were approaching the equator. Then he wondered how long it would be before he again saw that same star over their bows, rising higher and higher as they headed northward toward Britain and King Arthur's court in Camelot.

Camelot? King Arthur? Launcelot? Merry, prankish, ever-gay Sir Gawain? When would he see them again?

Fate played cruel tricks. Or was there a providence in all things, so that nothing that happened was without its good reason? The stars and the velvet sky and the whispering waves asked many questions and a troubled Val waited in vain for answers that never came.

South and west blew the wind, favoring them as they followed along the out-jutting western coast of Africa. Boltar studied his map and watched with a hawk's eye for the mouth of a certain great river.

They saw no other ships. Daily the heat increased. Their constant concern was to find drinking water along the desert shore. But none of the crew grumbled whether they found water or not, for their greed for gold overcame all pain and hardship. But one day a worse disaster struck.

It came without warning. It happened in this manner.

The wind suddenly died away. The air became thick, hot, stifling, so

that it was difficult to breathe. Then all sounds ceased and there was a frightening stillness which Val could liken only to the sepulchral stillness of death.

But most ominous of all were the massive brown clouds which now billowed up as if brought into being by a witch's curse, seeming to rise somewhere beyond the sandy shore where the Sahara stretched for endless miles.

Boltar and his Vikings gazed at these dire signs and portents with mouths agape and eyes white with fear. These hardy warriors who had faced mortal enemies with contempt a thousand times before, now quailed before the Unknown like the most craven of cowards. Nor did Val for all his courage fare any better. They all stared in terrible fascination.

The next instant it was as if all the screaming fiends of the lower world were released at once.

The sand storm rushed down upon them.

No one could face the wind, which slashed and stabbed with myriad tiny knives.

Their mast snapped like a dry reed. Before the fury of this onslaught the Vikings finally regained their senses. Some seized oars and strove as best they could to keep the ship's nose in the wind. The rest bailed like madmen or heaved ballast over the side. By these efforts they succeeded in staying upright. Nevertheless, before the storm had spent itself, they were

13

The lookout in the prow shouted that he saw
what he took to be a snow-capped peak ahead.

driven far out on the unknown ocean.

Despite the fact that they were driven so far off their course and their vessel was battered and leaking, they congratulated themselves upon their miraculous escape. But in their anxiety to outride the storm they had quite forgotten that they had exhausted their food and water. And now it came upon them with full force that thirst and starvation would soon complete what the storm had begun.

And here they were favored, as it seemed, with another stroke of good fortune. The lookout in the prow shouted excitedly that he saw what he took to be a snow-capped peak hard ahead. Val and Boltar, peering through the brownish, dusty haze—for the air was still filled with sandy particles swept up from the desert—agreed that this was correct. The crew then bent to the oars with a will, filled with anticipation of cool mountain streams, game of various sorts, and pleasant grassy slopes on which to rest. Indeed, rest and sleep were their immediate desires, since they had not shut their eyes all through the storm. But no sooner did they beach their ship on the mountainous island than a pack of monstrous dogs lined the shore.

By accident Val, Boltar and his Vikings had rediscovered the famous "Isle of Canines" or, as they are now known, the Canary Islands.

They fought past the wolfish dogs, killing many. The island was a paradise. They found water. They found cedar and oak and pine with which to repair their ship. But not for a moment could they shut their eyes, for the monstrous pack kept them surrounded, howling incessantly, their fangs gleaming. And so finally in desperation they sailed off, setting their course

eastward to the African coast, then south for many miles, then sharp east once again as the line of the great continent bent inward. Gradually the character of the country had been changing. In place of the vast, arid tree-less wastes there was now a lush luxuriance of tropic jungle coming down to the very edge of the sea. There were rivers, muddy, teeming, a riot of strange growths; and forest that grew in the sea itself. The heat was terrific. Boltar and Val took their turns at the oars, for no human strength was able for long to endure the endless withering heat.

At length Boltar sighted the mouth of a wide river, and after exclaim-

ing that this was the river indicated on the captain's map ordered his men to turn and row inland.

And here was a world of contrasts—sons of the icy northlands rowing a Viking ship through steaming, overgrown, fever-haunted jungles; hideous scaly dragons squirming on slimy mudbanks while gorgeous birds glided overhead; river monsters of nightmarish ugliness amongst water lilies; orchids growing in rotted stumps. Beauty and horror were everywhere.

As the vessel moved slowly up the river, enemies they could neither see nor fight attacked them. First it was fever. Then from the dense tangle along the banks came flights of stinging, poisoned darts causing festering wounds from which some of the men died.

Only the mad desire for gold kept these adventurers from turning back.

At dusk they reached a native village. But only to find it deserted. Val wondered why. Then he discovered the terrible answer. There was a movement among the trees. Seeing it Val darted forward. He burst through the

17

thicket and there, directly before him, loomed an ogre of such terrifying aspect that Val's blood turned to water in his veins.

The ogre's fangs, sharp as tusks, were bared. His eyes shone with such malevolence as only the demons of Satan could match. He remained motionless, fixing his glare on the young knight as if considering how most quickly to destroy him.

After his first fright Val recovered some measure of self-possession. Like the ogre himself, Val, too, remained motionless, deeming this wiser for the moment than either attack or flight. The monster stood at least six feet tall; in sheer bulk, however, he equalled four or five Viking warriors. As to his strength, and the power of his mighty arms, who could say? The black hair bristled out from his body.

Long years ago, in his boyhood in Thule, Val had heard travelers and hunters who came to his father's court tell of monsters like this . . . never seen alive or dead by any of them but only described to them by terrified tribesmen who feared these brutes more than they feared the wildest lions. Val could understand now why the village was deserted.

For an instant longer Val and the gigantic monster faced each other. Then he lifted his arms and beat his chest, and a sound like war drums echoed through the jungle. He moved slowly . . . and slowly Val gave ground, calling as he did so to Boltar and the men for aid.

Then the monster rushed, snarling hideously, his fangs clashing.

The Singing Sword flashed down. But the mighty stroke only wounded

and infuriated the horrible creature.

Before Val could lift his sword for another stroke, the wood-demon snatched his shield and threw it aside. Val saw the hairy arm coming. He ducked, but too late. Val was flung like a wet rag into the thicket.

By this time Boltar and his men were running up, beating their shields and yelling like fiends. The demon paused for only an instant then came on, moving with a weird swaying motion on his knuckled-under hands and his enormous handlike feet.

Boltar and his men hurled their spears at this fearful swaying target. The oncoming beast minded the spears no more than if they had been tiny pins.

The courage and reckless daring of the Vikings were beyond question. They rushed in to close with this enemy and met him head-on.

Some hacked at him mercilessly with battle-axes; others flailed him with broadswords, or plunged knives and daggers into his matted hide.

The beast roared with pain and rage. He seized a warrior and held him aloft, while the warrior screamed and his companions stood frozen with horror, unable to help. Then he dashed the man to the ground and trampled him. He seized another warrior and literally tore him to shreds.

Val, who had been stunned by his fall, now struggled painfully to his feet. Presently he was back in the thick of the fight. And at last the Singing Sword did its deadly work.

The ogre fell heavily and lay still, his evil eyes still glaring and his fangs gleaming as ferociously as in life.

Then, cautiously, came a nat.

from out of the jungle. By signs he made plain he was headman of the tribe
that had occupied the village. He thanked the white warriors for slaying
the wood-demon. But this slain monster was only one of many who were
now terrifying the villagers, devouring their crops, preventing them from
hunting, starving them all. Would the white warriors drive the monsters off?

A parley was now held. Val showed the headman the golden nuggets.
The headman returned answer that they had some and knew where to get
more. Then it was agreed that if the wood-demons were driven off, all the
gold that two of the strongest white warriors could lift together in a basket
would be given in payment.

And so, with the bargain fairly struck, Val set to work at once con-
structing small but powerful mangonels. These weapons could drive a spear
with shattering force, through rope and pulley tension on a prodigiously

strong bow. They were fortress weapons; they seemed right for this job.

Having set up the mangonels around the cleared ground where the crops were ripening, Val and the Vikings maintained vigilance. At dusk the monsters were seen moving at the edge of the jungle. Then they advanced and began feeding. Val signalled. The mangonels twanged.

A few of the wood-demons, struck squarely, fell dead. The rest, crazed with blood, turned and charged, roaring, snarling, tearing, battering. But Val and the Vikings held firm. The destruction was terrible, and not without its cost in human lives. In the end the demons fled. Native scouts watched them moving in a band to quieter regions. The next morning the headman sat in his village again. But shortly thereafter he set off up the river to get enough gold to fulfill his solemn bargain with the victorious white warriors,

for he had far too little on hand to satisfy Boltar.

Scarcely was the native canoe around the bend than Boltar spoke urgently: "Prince Val, follow them! See where they get the gold. To them gold means nothing. But for us it means a new life . . . an end to thieving and piracy!" More for adventure's sake than otherwise, Val consented to go.

So for the next several days Val and his tiny band warily followed the canoe upstream . . . until they reached the spot where the natives had banked the canoe, then trailed after them deep into the shadowy jungle.

Fearful were the dangers that beset the band. A unicorn charged into them and gored to death one of them. And at twilight, as they made ready to camp, a fantastic brown-flecked horned serpent—or could it be a long-necked animal?—reared its head above the treetops. They would have fled

in panic only that they feared worse terrors than these in the jungle at night.

None of them slept that night. But the greatest terror of all came the next morning shortly after dawn.

They were making ready to break camp and were filling their skins at a nearby water hole when they were startled by a rumbling noise that they first mistook for distant thunder.

Then the ground beneath their feet began to thud and shudder. They stiffened with that overpowering fear that grips even the bravest men during an earthquake; for that is what they were certain it was.

Suddenly they heard the heavy tramp of footsteps. Branches snapped and cracked around them. Monkeys leaped. Birds flew off screaming.

Then they beheld it . . . and stopped breathing!

They knew then that what towered before them must be the marvel and the monarch of all creation . . . a beast beside which the giant wood-demons were as pygmies. So mammoth was it that it seemed unfair to humans, in the same proportion and for the same reason that humans must seem unfair to worms and gnats.

They were struck with wonder of the legs, each the thickness of the trunk of an oak tree. The great winged ears and the enormous ivory tusks, sharp-pointed like spears, made them gasp in incredulity.

But what awed them most was the serpentine nose which wound itself around a tree and pulled it up by the roots as though it were a weed, then sent it crashing upon them.

They turned and fled.

They went rushing
headlong back along
the jungle path, sure
that each moment
would be their last.

Boltar and his mate
lifted the leathern
basket strung on a
bamboo pole and the
gold was theirs!

They stopped once to hurl their spears and shoot a flight of arrows at the beast. Val drew the Singing Sword and thrust viciously at its underbelly. Striking the leathery hide the spears and arrows fell harmlessly to the ground. Val's deadly blade hardly made a scratch. They went rushing headlong back along the jungle path up which they had come, sure that each moment would be their last.

On reaching the edge of the river they dragged their boat into the water and rowed furiously downstream, leaving the awesome monster on the bank, trumpeting shrilly.

Val heaved a sigh of relief when once again he and his companions stepped ashore at the native village.

Boltar expressed himself as disappointed that they had returned without finding the source of the gold. "There comes a time," Val said curtly, "when gold costs more than it is worth." Boltar grimaced, but he understood. Two days later the natives returned, their canoe well laden with golden nuggets.

And so the hour of payment to the white warriors for driving off the wood-demons arrived. Boltar came all prepared with a capacious leathern basket strung on a stout bamboo pole. He also came with his first mate, a man almost as strong as Boltar himself. Then the chieftain heaped the basket with gold and bade them lift it, and keep it if they could.

Boltar well nigh broke his back and the mate suffered from strained tendons the rest of his life. But the basket was lifted and the gold theirs!

Then into the ship they all piled, and away! Past the wallowing river monsters they sped, out into the open sea. Then they shouted for joy—

Day after day they strained at the oars with never a favoring wind.

But the shouts of joy at being on the open sea again soon changed to groans as day after day they strained at the oars with never a favoring wind. Finally, off North Spain, they picked up the "westerlies" and went foaming across the Bay of Biscay to the Gaulish shore. Here Boltar put in at the nearest port for supplies. A frowning castle dominated the town.

That night as Val and Boltar were in an inn making their first farewells—for by the morrow Val would be home—a castle courtier approached

A castle courtier approached Val and Boltar in an inn and offered Boltar a purse to take a letter to Britain.

and offered Boltar a purse to take a letter to Britain. Boltar agreed; but as soon as the courtier left he broke the seal and pushed the letter at Val. "I mistrust writing, Valiant. Read what it says." Val looked at it, then let out an oath. "It's a demand for ransom for my friend Sir Gawain. The master of the castle holds him a prisoner in his dungeon. Give me my share of the gold nuggets. I'll ransom him myself."

Marvelously joyous was the embrace of the two old friends the next

29

morning when the dungeon doors swung open and a handsome, slightly pale knight swaggered out. Then Gawain, free of his chains, and Prince Val, free of his hard-won gold, strode laughing and singing and altogether hilarious and impoverished, out of the castle bailey and out through the tower gate and over the rattling drawbridge and into the sunshine of freedom . . . and hunger.

"And why shouldn't we be happy, my fine Prince?" queried Gawain. "We are alive, are we not? Can you give me a sounder reason for being happy?" Then, when Val smiled instead of answering, Gawain went merrily on: "And mark you this, a man being alive may be in tatters one day and in silk the next. And there is love . . . now is it not largely true that it is the lad with empty pockets and a daring heart who always wins the princess?"

A look came over Val's face; for Gawain's words had painfully evoked the memory of Aleta. Gawain, quick to notice he had said something amiss, changed his tone. "Well," he said briskly, "let us find this Viking captain of yours and hie us home to Camelot."

But it was not to be "home to Camelot" for quite a while yet for Val and Gawain. Boltar, being impatient to spend some of his gold in his own land and feeling confident that the two knights would easily find another ship to take them across the channel, sailed off.

"No matter," said Gawain to Val. "I suddenly recall that we need not

worry about where we shall eat and sleep. I quite forgot Sir Hubert."

"Sir Hubert? Who is he, Gawain?"

"An excellent knight of excellent liberality and excellent wealth. The only drawback is that his castle is . . . sixty excellent miles away."

Laughing again they set out for Sir Hubert's castle.

Val found Sir Hubert as jovial and generous as Gawain had pictured him. He ate well, lived well, and loved all around him to do the same. "Stay to your heart's content," he welcomed them. "Sir Gawain, you look pale. We will put color back in your face. Sir Valiant, you look sad, like a poet with none to appreciate his roundels. We will see that you meet some fair listeners with roguish eyes before whom your verse will not be wasted."

Thus nearly a month passed pleasantly. Then one night came a pounding at the door and a lady with frightened eyes was ushered in. "Lady Anne of Gaiforte!" Sir Hubert exclaimed. "You come with bad news."

The Lady Anne told a strange story. "My husband Robert has been spirited away, no one knows where. My servants tell of witches and demons in the woods at night . . . weird cries, flickering lights. None will help me."

Hereupon Val and Gawain drew their swords and took solemn oath to find Robert, Thane of Gaiforte. Next morning they escorted the Lady Anne back to Castle Gaiforte. "Now," said Val to the Lady Anne as they were riding, "I don't put too much stock in witches and demons. Did your

"I ask the questions, not you," Givric retorted. "On guard!"

husband have any enemies who might have wanted to get rid of him?"

Lady Anne replied: "Only one—Givric, sheriff of Boisvert."

"When a man's friends don't know where he is, his enemies generally do. Let's pay a visit to this Givric," Val said to Gawain. To this Gawain readily consented, so upon leaving the Lady Anne safe in her castle at Gaiforte, they repaired at once to the nearby castle of the sheriff of Boisvert. Gawain pounded on the gate. Presently a man-at-arms appeared. "Tell your master to come forth," Gawain said. "We have a question for him."

Val and Gawain had only a few minutes to wait for Givric, sheriff of Boisvert, to come raging out, mounted, fully accoutred and ready for battle. "Which of you has the insolence to summon me to answer questions?"

"I do, in the name of the Lady Anne of Gaiforte!" shouted Gawain.

"I ask the questions, not you," Givric retorted. "On guard!"

Both men wheeled about, steadied their lances, then came thundering toward each other. In the clash that followed the next instant both lances were splintered to the very grip. Though dazed by the blow, each knight managed to keep his seat.

Gawain and Givric had both drawn their swords and were preparing to continue the fight when Val called "Hold!" and rode in between them. He spoke to Gawain, saying: "This Givric is a hearty knight. He may slay us both, or either of us may slay him before we learn the fate of Robert."

"The fate of Robert of Gaiforte?" echoed Givric in consternation. "He is my enemy, as all know. Yet before some angry words were spoken between us he was my dearest friend. Has some ill befallen him?"

On hearing the story, Givric shook his head. "I know nothing to account for Robert's disappearance. . . . Or perhaps I do," he hinted darkly a moment later. "Maybe the 'Curse of Blacktower' has returned." He led the way to a high turret and pointed across the somber forest.

In the distance a blackened ruin rose stark above the trees. "That is Blacktower . . . a haunted place," Givric said. "One night, more than twenty years ago, the castle was set afire and all perished but the mistress of Blacktower and her baby girl. Robert's father was blamed, for he and the master of Blacktower were bitter foes. A curse was laid on Robert's father and all his descendants . . . the curse of Blacktower—"

Givric described other eerie details about Blacktower, how screams had been lately heard coming from within its charred walls. "For me," Gawain interrupted, "this quest is ended. I draw the line at fighting ghosts and hobgoblins."

"Nevertheless, tomorrow we visit Blacktower," said Val. "All this is too fantastic to be true." But it still took a good deal of persuasion before Gawain reluctantly agreed to go with Val to Blacktower. They reached it late the next afternoon. Leaving their superstitious squires outside the ruined gates, they drew a deep breath and ventured in alone.

The courtyard glowed red from the sinking sun. They entered the crumbling, almost roofless tower. High overhead among the black rafters bats fluttered with muted wings.

A terrifying scream shattered the unearthly silence. The echoes awoke, rushed about wildly. Gradually silence returned.

They could hear the loud beating of their hearts. Suddenly in the far wall a door swung open.

In the fiery glow of the sunset stood a slim maid, silent, motionless.

Then she spoke, and in speaking broke the frightful spell. "Thank Heaven for sending me two stalwart knights. Your help comes none too soon." She glided over to where they stood. "A beautiful tragic face," Val thought. "She has suffered much."

The maid was saying: "My brother and I have been living in this accursed place. The horror of it has made him quite mad. You must help me get him out. Come—"

They followed her into a passage

where, hearing a click, they saw her turn a key and lock the door behind them. "I do so," she explained, "that my poor addled brother may not rush out and do himself harm. Stand guard here. I will return with him." They saw her go out past the door at the other end of the passage . . . then with a cry Val leaped forward. But too late. She had already locked this door as well. Then she backed away, the somber eyes burning with insane hate. It did no good to call after her. She glided up the stairs and was gone, leaving them imprisoned and in almost total darkness. They had been tricked into the dungeon. "I was a fool," Val blamed himself. "I followed her because I thought she would lead us to Robert of Gaiforte."

Here they fancied they heard a voice whispering: "And you have found me." Peering across the passage they made out another prisoner, his face pressed against the bars of his cell. "I am Robert of Gaiforte," he said. "The maid duped me as she has duped you. She is the daughter of my father's

old foe Dieman, the Lord of Blacktower, who died years ago in this flaming castle. My father was blamed, cursed. She is possessed by the mad idea that she must perpetuate the curse of Blacktower by burning me alive . . ."

During the night, hearing the sound of shuffling footsteps, Val and Gawain noiselessly looked out into the passage. There they saw a hideous old hag descending the stairs with a bundle of dry branches. She cackled as she heaped the wood in a corner and went up for more. "For a fire," Gawain said uncomfortably, not relishing the idea of being roasted alive in a cell. "That old hag's got the key—"

Val nodded. He waited until she passed again, then he shot out his arms and pinned her back against the outside of the cell. A dagger slashed across his fingers . . . but not before he had seized the key and snatched off a hideous mask. The "old hag" was the crazed maid of Blacktower. She raged at them: "You have the key, but you cannot reach the lock!"

37

With the key speared on a kerchief, like bait on a line, Val fished for the outside keyhole.

She burst into maniacal laughter. "Yes, I am the daughter of Dieman of Blacktower, last of my race, a child of wrath! Robert of Gaiforte, cursed by my father, must die in fire and be purified. And you meddling knights will die with him like pigs!" She went off to get more fuel and a torch.

With the key speared on a kerchief, like bait on a line, Val fished for the outside keyhole . . . then found it and slotted the key home. This done, a harder problem now waited; how to turn the out-of-reach key in the lock? A lever would do it. But where find a lever? "The Singing Sword!" cried Val.

So the great battle-hardened sword was balanced from another kerchief and coaxed until it slid into the narrow eye of the key. Then the key was turned and the door of the cell flung open. They darted across the passageway to Robert's cell. But the same key would not open his door.

From the head of the stairs the crazed daughter of Dieman saw them frantically trying to free Robert. She had a blazing torch now. She threw it into the pile of dry wood. Then, when the flames leaped up, she fled, climbing high into the tower, singing crazily, hurling down broken stones.

The passageway had flared into an inferno. From inside his cell Robert of Gaiforte pleaded pitifully: "Save yourselves, brave knights! Why should we all three die? Go while there is yet time!"

Heedless, the two knights stayed, and in the choking passage found a heavy timber which they rammed with the strength of desperation against

When the flames leaped
up, she fled, climbing
high into the tower,
singing crazily, hurling
down broken stones.

39

Robert's door until it crashed and the half-dead prisoner staggered out. Then they battered down the last remaining door shutting them in the passageway and gained the open courtyard. A shriek made them look up. On the brink of the flaming tower stood Dieman's daughter, dancing a macabre dance of death . . . then the tower sank into the flames, and she with it.

On the brink of the flaming tower stood Dieman's daughter, dancing a macabre dance of death.

Then the tower sank into the flames, and she with it.

It was dawn when they set out for Castle Gaiforte, supporting the helpless Robert between them. They had still far to go when they were rewarded by the sight of Givric, who had seen the flames from afar and had come to learn their fate. Though he feigned indifference to his former friend, he consented stiffly to enter Gaiforte which he had resolutely shunned for the

past five years in petulant remembrance of what, for anyone else, would have been a forgotten quarrel.

For a long moment the Lady Anne and Robert held each other close, not caring who saw their tears of happiness. But when Givric would have slipped away, feeling in his pride that he was still an enemy, they would not let him go. And so it turned out that Val and Gawain, riding forth from Castle Gaiforte a little while later, had the pleasure of seeing that their quest had succeeded not only in bringing husband and wife together but in restoring two bitter enemies to a friendship they might have lost forever.

This done, Val and Gawain pointed their horses' heads northward across Brittany, determined not to stop until they reached the English Channel whence they could sail the last few rough miles separating them from home. Thus they drew near a peaceful castle; but were astonished on enter-

"Somehow," said Val, as they rode into the midst of the warriors, "half these men look familiar to me."

A great voice was roaring: "Prince Val, my sprouting knight!" and Val needed no second look to see who it was.

ing the town at the castle's foot to come on a furious battle raging in the streets.

"Ah, a welcome sight," said Gawain, getting sword and lance ready.

"Somehow," said Val, narrowing his eyes as they rode into the midst of the warriors, "half these men look familiar to me. Where did I see them before?"

As Val said this, suddenly their horses were encircled by bronzed Vikings, and a great voice was roaring: "Prince Val, my sprouting knight!"

Val needed no second look to see who it was. "Boltar!" he cried. "You respectable old merchant and honest pirate! I might have known from the hullabaloo that you were in town!"

Seeing that the Viking chief and his ferocious warriors were now otherwise occupied, the townspeople and castle men-at-arms who had been striving to drive them off, quietly backed away to await developments.

43

While this was happening, Boltar had yanked Val off his horse and after giving him a hug to crush a granite pillar, demanded to know how he fared. Val described their recent adventures, then said: "And if you have finished your business dealings here, Boltar, Sir Gawain and I will voice no serious nay to allowing an honest pirate such as . . . ahem you, to ferry us across the channel." Boltar laughed deeply, gathered his men together, waved farewell to the relieved townsmen and soldiers, and the next morning set the two knights safely ashore by the cheerful white cliffs of Britain. Then the lovable old rogue took leave at last, vowing to see them again unless he had the ill-luck to be hanged first. And so, a few days later, Val and Gawain saw Camelot once more towering in wonderful grace before them.

44

Setting spurs to their mounts they clattered through the Merlin Gate at full gallop, and a shout of welcome went up. For Val had been gone for three years and many in Camelot had feared never to see him alive again.

Val at once presented himself before King Arthur and his queen. The king's voice was solemn. "We now bid adieu to peace and quiet. In addition, we command that everything breakable be put away. Prince Valiant has returned!" Then joy sparkled in Arthur's eyes and he bade Val be welcome. That night all the fellowship of the Round Table gathered for a feast. But when the merrymaking had died down, King Arthur rose and announced grave news. "The savage Northmen and Picts have grown turbulent again and threaten our northern borders. Prepare you for war."

In the days that followed Val trained with all the rough gusto of healthy youth. From dawn to dusk the fields of Camelot rang with the clash of arms; of lances, broadswords, battle-axes and plain fists. Some knights received wounds that laid them low for weeks; but at length King Arthur saw that they were growing hard, accurate, and would soon be ready.

Then he called Prince Valiant to his side and said: "We have a dangerous mission for you. Many years ago, when the Romans ruled Britain, a great wall was built across the northern marches from sea to sea to hold back the border tribes. It is our desire that you see if this wall can be put in repair and once more used for defense. You will select a companion-knight to ride with you, so that should one come to grief, the other may live to return." Val at once named Sir Gawain to accompany him.

To Val's surprise Gawain seemed somewhat less than pleased with the mission. Nevertheless they both rode out of Camelot and struck northward. The winter was severe and it grew steadily colder. And all this time Val noticed with pain the unwelcome change that had come over the usually gay Gawain. Then one day Gawain refused to go further. "The wall?" he said. "Everyone knows it is a crumbling rock pile. Why must we suffer months of hardship to discover what is already known? You may go on if you like. As for me, I know a snug castle where I will spend the winter."

Val rode on with a heavy heart, followed now only by his squire, looking back often, half-hoping Gawain was only joking and would soon come galloping up; laughing that Val should have been fooled into thinking him

46

undutiful to his king. But this was not to be.

Val followed the old Roman road without difficulty; it was still well-marked despite the wear and weathering of more years and more generations than anyone could remember. Occasionally, but more rarely as he kept pushing northward, he would meet peasants and shepherds, or pass tiny hamlets made up of half a dozen miserable thatched huts. The people who came out to stare at him showed themselves more and more hostile. But not as yet, seeing him to be strongly armed, did they venture to attack.

Val now came upon one of the unexplainable curiosities of olden days: a huge ditch extending over hill and valley as far as the eye could see. To this day people are wondering why the Romans dug the "vallum."

Then finally from a high ledge he saw the wall, and he marvelled how even Rome, in the massive fullness of its military might, could have conceived and executed so vast a work. At every mile, and for mile after mile, along the route of the wall there had been built a great stone fortress. And between each fortress and the next there were two signal towers; so that commands and alarms travelled from tower to tower in minutes over distances which not even the swiftest courier could ride in days.

That night Val and his squire made camp in one of the deserted fortresses. Val had caught some game. Soon a cheerful fire was crackling in what must once have been a hearth, and they ate with keen appetite.

It was some time later that night that the strange thing happened. Indeed, for once Val, who was not ordinarily given to superstition, was ready to believe what his eyes seemed to see . . . and what his eyes seemed to see was a visitor from the time long past when the Roman legions were quartered here in all the fortresses along the wall.

It came about in this manner. Val and his squire, having finished their meal, had brushed the embers from the ledge of the hearth and stretched themselves out on the still-warm stones. They had built another small fire on the stone floor for the night. It was time for sleep.

But sleep did not come to Val. He lay restlessly awake, watching the shadows as they crouched in the deep recesses . . . creeping out, darting back . . . dancing in dark mysterious rhythm to the flickering fire. To Val's mind thronged disturbing memories: of Aleta whose face still haunted him; of Gawain who seemed to be disowning all that was fine in his heart. And suddenly—

Val stared. He saw it plainly. He roused his squire. "Look! The ghost

Julian told them a tale
of devotion to duty.

Julian had been wounded by
the fighting on the wall.

The wall was left
in his care.

He kept perpetual
guard upon it.

The duty passed on
to his eldest son.

of a Roman centurion! But how can this be? Not for half a century has a Roman soldier been in Britain!"

Then the "ghost" spoke, telling Val and the squire a strange tale of devotion to duty. "In the year 412 Rome recalled her Legions from Britain. But Julian, a centurion, could not leave with the others, having just been wounded unto death by the fighting on the wall. His officer said: 'Farewell, brave Julian. We must leave the wall in your care until we return.' But Julian did not die. Remembering his officer's words, he kept perpetual guard upon the wall . . . and when he grew too old, he passed the sacred duty on to his eldest son. And thus you find me, another Julian, but still the guardian of the wall." When Julian learned from Val that King Arthur would repair the ancient wall and defend it against the fierce Picts, he smiled: "The Julians have obeyed, and now their work is done."

Early the next morning Val, Julian and Val's squire set out on a tour of the wall. Julian led the way. At once Val realized how valuable a helper he was; for though they passed hostile tribes of Picts in the villages along the wall, all stood respectfully aside as Julian strode boldly by.

And so, thanks to this descendant of Romans, Val moved safely across Britain from the Tyne to Solway Firth. Val dispatched his trusty squire back to Camelot with the information so far obtained. For Val would trust none but himself on his next mission. In spite of Julian's advice he scaled the wall and started travelling still further northward. He had stripped off his armor. Somewhere among the rugged Scottish hills Val hoped to

They set out on a tour of the wall. Julian led the way.

51

discover the hidden invasion force of the Viking Northmen. He was certain their allies the Picts knew. For several days Val was allowed to travel northward unmolested. He was "allowed" because the band of Pict warriors who, unseen, had been watching and following, deemed it best to let him ensnare himself deep within their territory before they seized him. He looked dangerous.

But at length they decided he had gone far enough.

Val was ascending a misty hillside when a circle of Picts arose from the heather. The first of the men made at him with a battle-ax; Val buried his spear in the man's ribs, then whirled around, reaching for his short sword to meet the onslaught. He never had a chance to draw the sword. A few minutes later, securely bound and disarmed, he was forced to march.

The way led over the wild and beautiful hills toward the sea. Val grit his teeth in silent rage. He would find the Viking force now. And there it was, the entire fleet, drawn up along the shore of a narrow sheltered bay!

Val was brought at once before an old foe: Horsa, the indomitable sea rover. He waited to see if the Viking chief recognized him. Apparently he did not. "Why do you bother to capture a simple peasant like me?" Val asked innocently. But Horsa was not so easily fooled.

"Can an eagle parade as a crow?" Horsa said angrily. "You are one of Arthur's knights. Now tell me why you spy among these alien hills?" And when Val remained stubbornly silent, Horsa said: "Perhaps we can loosen your tongue." He ordered his men to put the prisoner to the rack.

It took a good dozen of them to drag Val off, for he kicked like a wild

52

Securely bound and disarmed, he was forced to march.

Val grit his teeth in silent rage.

stallion. But fight or no, Prince Val was tied to the instrument of torment. Then once more and for the last time the wrathful Viking sea rover exhorted Val to confess the reasons for his spying and to acknowledge his identity as one of Arthur's knights.

To all this Val jeered, urging Horsa to do his worst.

"As you wish," the Viking said, and signalled his torturer to begin.

Now the tale tells that while Val was being thus fiendishly used in expectation that the pain to his racked limbs would compel his lips to spill out their secrets, Sir Gawain was suffering torture of another kind though not, perhaps, much less painful.

After having parted company with his young companion near the northern marches some weeks before through refusing to undergo further (and, as he said then) unnecessary hardships, Gawain had taken himself to a castle not far off whose master was known to offer gaiety and carousing to any pleasant company who might venture by. For a time this was exactly to Gawain's mood . . . then a small voice within him began reminding him that he deserved disgrace and banishment for thus forswearing his fealty to his king . . . for letting Val endure all peril alone . . . for shaming the proud name of the knightly fellowship of the Round Table. At last he could still this relentless and merciless inner voice no longer. With scant apologies to his merry but self-indulgent host, he abruptly armed and rode off, northward.

And so at length, after many adventures of his own along the way, it is related that Gawain came to the edge of the Viking camp on the day and at the hour that Val was being broken. But he was witness to even greater horrors; for the rack, having proved ineffectual, was discarded . . . and Horsa's torturer had set about heating up some irons. . . .

54

*There was one sentry
when Gawain came.*

There was nothing for Gawain to
do but wait, and pray, that Val would
hold on to what little was left of his
life . . . until nightfall.

And so it was. With the coming of
dusk, Horsa called a halt to the day's
ghastly sport so that something might
remain for the morrow. Gawain, ey-
ing every move of the fierce warriors,
saw them carrying the unconscious
prince toward the ships. But he dared
not follow. In agony he waited for
darkness. When it came, he moved
with superlative cunning and match-
less courage.

Armed only with a dagger, he entered the icy waters of the bay, and
swam toward the beached Viking
ships. A low moan led him to the
lonely spot where Val was shuddering
under a heap of furs. There was but
one sentry on duty when Gawain
came; there was but one sentry, but
no longer on duty, when Gawain dis-
appeared back into the sea dragging
Val after him. Then began the homeward journey beset with all manner of

*The homeward
journey was
beset with
all manner
of perils.*

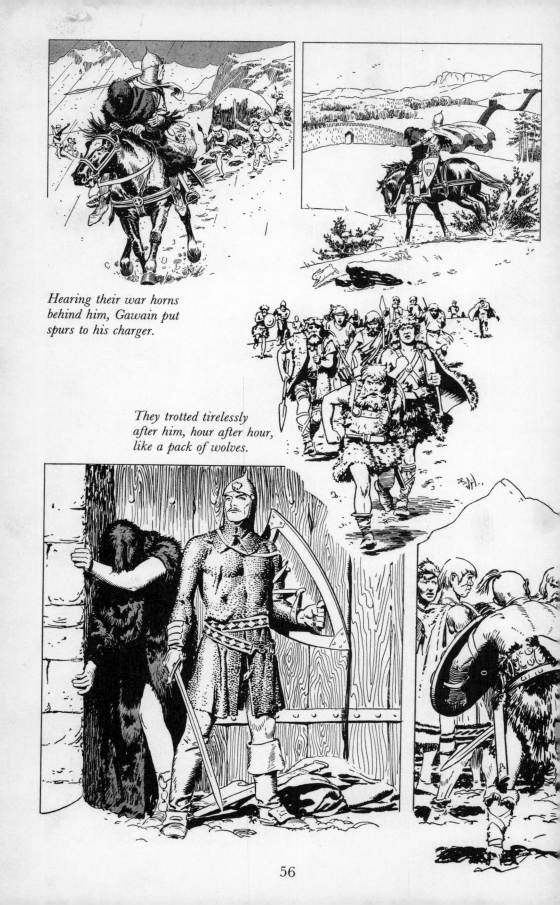

Hearing their war horns
behind him, Gawain put
spurs to his charger.

They trotted tirelessly
after him, hour after hour,
like a pack of wolves.

perils of which the icy Highland winds were not the worst.

Though he had regained consciousness and was aware that Gawain had spared him further torture, Val cared little if he lived or died. He burned with fever. His wounds made him groan with every step of the tired horse over the uneven ground. And when pain grew too piercing for human endurance he lapsed back into merciful unconsciousness. Thus they went on.

But it was the bands of savage Picts who threatened most. As word of the escape spread, the Picts promised their Viking allies to retake the two knights. They scoured the countryside, hill and glen, and soon spied them heading for the old Roman wall. Hearing their war horns behind him, Gawain put spurs to his charger, but could not shake them off. They trotted tirelessly after him, hour after hour, like a pack of wolves.

At last, with joy, Gawain beheld the long Roman wall rising just ahead. Like Val, he too had encountered the centurion Julian and learned of the deathless tradition of the Guardian of the Gate. It was toward the fortress gate that Gawain now raced, hoping that Julian might be there to open it. He shouted . . . there was no sound save only the howls of the oncoming Picts. Gawain had lifted Val off the horse; and now with Val protected behind him, he drew his sword. Then the gate opened wide. Julian stepped forth, stern, forbidding, like one of the great Caesars. The Picts fell back, murmuring in superstitious awe: "The Deathless One . . ." and did not move when Val was carried through the gate to Julian's cottage. There the

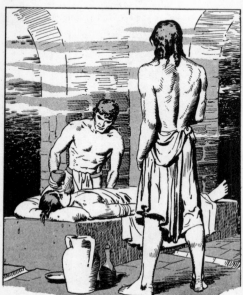

frightful wounds were cleansed and dressed; and the ancient Roman steam
room did good work still; yet nothing helped so much as the warmth and
love in Julian's home. Then with spring in the air again, Val tried his legs

and found them steady. So he took leave of these friends (and was not ashamed to let his tears be seen), and rode the long miles with Gawain at his side, until once more his squire was greeting him in Camelot. But when King Arthur saw the scars of Viking torture on Val's body, his fury knew no bounds; then he assembled his knights and let them likewise see what twisted savagery had done so that they roared: "Lead us against the Vikings!"—and

straightway mounted their chargers and started northward that very day with King Arthur riding grim and silent at their head. But Val, still far from

Val was put in the care of Morgan Todd.

healed, was put in the care of famed Morgan Todd, the king's own physician. None in all Britain excelled this Morgan Todd in the healing art and only half his cures were based on superstition; so that, in being left with him, Val was left in the best of hands, as indeed proved to be the case.

But Morgan Todd was not Val's only physician. With all the other knights away to war, it was not strange that this handsome youth should have been mothered and sistered by more winsome nurses than any convalescent rightly needs. But Morgan Todd was too shrewd a physician not to know that laughter and flirtation and merry words can often mend better than all your pills and plaisters.

It was not long, therefore, before Morgan Todd pronounced Val sound and able. Val thanked the good doctor, told him he agreed with him heartily and went at once with his squire into the exercise yard where he shook most of the stiffness out of his joints by playfully swinging a two-headed ax.

Next day at dawn Val was out in the exercise yard again with his squire. Now they both donned training pads, shields, helmets and breastplates, and went at each other with short swords.

"Well done," said Val after several bouts in this fashion; "though I am by way of thinking you used less force against me than you might have. What? Do you consider me still weak?"

"Heaven help me if all my enemies are as weak as you," replied the squire, rubbing the side of his head.

An hour later Val was ready to leave Camelot. He thanked Morgan Todd. He kissed all the ladies farewell, and vowed solemnly to be true to each of them.

He and his squire rode northward, steadily, without pause through all the hours of daylight and often through the night as well. All traces of

playfulness faded from his eyes. For he had not forgotten the tortures of the Vikings, and hatred seared like a flame in his heart. And at length he caught up with King Arthur's forces and found them gathered behind a breach in the old Roman wall.

On the opposite side of the wall, guarded by a strong barricade, waited Horsa's Vikings with their savage allies, the Picts.

For a full week now Arthur's men and their foes had faced each other, jeering and gibing, yet neither daring to attack. Arthur's men were too few to charge headlong into the vast enemy horde. For should the attack be turned into a rout, the way would be open for the barbarians to swarm into Britain. For his part Horsa was suspicious of what forces might be lying secretly behind Arthur or to his flanks. So, like a crouching tiger the Viking chieftain waited patiently for his wily foe to make a rash move.

Then out stepped Thundaar, champion of the Northmen, and taunted from across the wall: "Frightened sheep, send forth a champion to feel the edge of my battle-ax! Or is there none among you who cares to fight?"

It was at this moment that Val rode up and started climbing wearily from his horse. But Thundaar's voice was like a refreshment. Instantly Val shouted back: "Viking windbag, I accept your challenge!" Then he leaped down from the wall and advanced carelessly, insolently, and without bothering to wear a helmet.

"Come back, Prince Valiant!" roared King Arthur. "I forbid you to fight! You are not yet well!" But Val seemed suddenly hard of hearing.

Arthur's men and their
foes faced each other,
jeering and gibing.

Thundaar taunted, "Is
there none among you
who cares to fight?"

The Singing Sword came whispering from its sheath.

In Thundaar's hands the battle-ax was not slow.

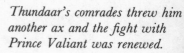

Val's shield remained low, his sword flicked upward . . . and the ax-handle was neatly sliced.

Thundaar's comrades threw him another ax and the fight with Prince Valiant was renewed.

Then the gleaming Singing Sword came whispering happily from its sheath, and the duel began. Thundaar was no bogus champion as Val soon saw, but deft, cool, tricky as a snake. The battle-ax, though more powerful than the sword, is somewhat slower. But in Thundaar's hands it was far from slow. For a few moments both opponents tested, searching out weaknesses.

Thundaar had one trick which up to now had proved fatal to all rivals. Horsa, watching from the Viking lines and knowing the trick was coming, smiled with his eyes; while King Arthur on the opposite side, frowned.

Thundaar's ax came up as if for a straight downward stroke, and he hesitated, waiting for Val to raise his shield and cover his eyes. For in that instant the great ax would reverse its direction in a staggering underhand swing. But Val sensed the feint. The shield remained low, the sword flicked upward . . . and the ax-handle was neatly sliced. Thundaar stood unarmed, looking foolish. His comrades threw him another ax and the fight was renewed. But in his blind rage Thundaar was easily led into using his now familiar trick. He raised the ax for a mighty blow. This time Val deliberately lifted his shield and decoyed Thundaar into making the furious underhand stroke. But as the arm shot down, the Singing Sword flicked out. Again the battle-ax flew into the air, and Thundaar's hand flew with it, still grasping.

Val strode back to his wildly cheering lines, while from the Viking side came only groans. But for Thundaar his fighting days were over. Val heard

Thundaar raised the ax for a mighty blow.

Val decoyed him into the furious stroke.

The ax flew into the air, the hand with it.

Val strode back to his wildly cheering lines.

his name called and discovered King Arthur gazing at him with an expression half-scowl, half-smile. The king said: "You seem to suffer from a most convenient deafness when our commands don't please you. Perhaps you would like to lead our army?"—"Yes sir!" replied Val with a disarming smile. "Let me have an army of just ten audacious horsemen and we will starve out the Vikings in a week by raiding their supply lines."

And so it was that Horsa's supply trains, keeping safely to the valleys, were struck again and again (but never twice in the same place) by armed horsemen who swooped down on them from the hills. They came, they

The Picts could not trap the marauders.

struck, they burnt, smashed, maimed . . . and they were gone!

Then many a Viking warrior began to suffer the pangs of hunger because of them, until finally Horsa was obliged to go to his allies the Picts to beg food. And the Picts, having all too little for themselves, were anything

*Val descried a Viking supply
train getting ready to camp
for the night.*

but pleased to have to divide their little into less. Then the Picts sent out scouts to trap the marauders, but they found only where they had been and never where they were.

From a lofty crag Val descried a large Viking supply train getting ready to camp for the night. Far off, in another direction, he made out a group of Pict scouts, the same who were searching for them. An idea now occurred to Val. Calling his men together, he said, "Mount and ride out into the open where the Picts can plainly see you. I want them attracted thither."

This was forthwith done and the Picts, greatly excited over having discovered the marauding knights, began at once, and cautiously, to move toward the place where they saw them. Hereupon the knights slipped away and rejoined their young leader. Nevertheless the Picts kept creeping forward, which was as Val wished.

Then the plan continued as follows: At midnight Val led his troop to the sleeping Viking supply train. They fell upon the defenders, slew all but two, and fled into the darkness taking the two Vikings with them as prisoners. But on this occasion Val was careful to leave all the supplies intact, as though he had been frightened off before being able to destroy them. Hardly had the troop gone than the Pict scouts came upon the raided Viking camp. Knowing the value of the supplies, they at once started gathering them up before the knights should return for them.

They fell upon the defenders.

"See?" said Val to his companions, but in a voice loud enough for the two Viking prisoners to overhear. "Our good friends the Picts have found the Viking stores we promised to leave for them. Now they will aid us by betraying Horsa." Not a word of this was true of course.

And stranger still, the two Viking prisoners happened to be so poorly bound that they escaped, and dashed off to tell Horsa what they had just learned of the perfidy of their trusted Pict allies. Then Val and his band of

daredevils rode back to their lines. "See," said Val to King Arthur, "our enemies now hate each other more than they do us. Let us peacefully withdraw and let them eliminate each other." And thus it happened. The allies fell out and fought; and finally the Vikings sailed home.

Val did not return to Camelot but wandered afield, a moody young prince. Suddenly, unbelievably, he came on just such a scene as he had encountered long ago in the Misty Isles: a maid washing her golden hair under a waterfall. Half beside himself with emotion Val called out: "Aleta!"

73

The girl turned, a simpering peasant lass, and Val rode unhappily on. Then he said to himself: "I shall go to the witch Horrit in the fens and learn if this bitter remembrance of Aleta is to be my fate forever . . ."

At the cottage of a boyhood friend Val stabled his charger; and in a borrowed dugout and swamp-shoes slithered through the mazes of the vast wasteland. With every faculty on the alert he was ready for the inevitable meeting with Horrit's fearsome son Thorg . . . and suddenly Thorg rose

The girl turned, a simpering peasant lass, and Val rode unhappily on.

In a borrowed dugout and swamp-shoes Val slithered through the vast wasteland.

over him. In that instant the naked blade of the Singing Sword formed a glittering barrier between them. Neither moved.

Then Val said in a quiet voice that held menace in its very quietness: "Easy, Thorg. I come as a generous client to your mother, or as a deadly enemy to you. Choose!" Mumbling, the great hulking terror of the fens turned and led the way to his mother's hut.

So wild and desolate and grim and foreboding was the scene that Val's heart was filled with dread. Nevertheless he clenched his teeth and started to enter the hut. But Horrit barred his way, pointing a bony hand at the Singing Sword, her eyes wild with horror. " 'Tis Flamberge, the accursed blade!" she cried. "Take it from my sight!"

Val hung sword-belt and sword handily outside, for he knew she would not treat with him otherwise. At length she consented to let him in.

They sat before the blazing fire. "See, princess of evil, I bring precious gifts for you and your fine son. I seek your wisdom.... Am I always to be under Aleta's spell? Am I nevermore to know contentment? Tell me."

Then Horrit cackled, while her loathsome Thorg gibbered hideously, and Val's scalp was like a tightening cap.

"Fool!" said the witch to Val. "Man suffers enough with memories of his past. Thrice cursed is he who knows his future."

The wrinkled, old haggish face pressed close to his. She went on: "Contentment is a gift beyond price, too rich for many a king yet often the only wealth of the meanest of beggars. Again I read your future. Too bad. For again I see adventure, wealth, much turmoil, but nowhere any contentment! None! None!"

"Fool!" said the witch to Val. "Man suffers enough with memories."

"'Tis Flamberge, the accursed blade! Take it from my sight!"

The wrinkled, old haggish face pressed close to his.

Sick at heart, Val fled from the hut with Horrit's baleful words still ringing in his ears. He found his dugout and made his way out of the unwholesome fen as quickly as he was able. Then he retrieved his charger and continued on, letting the horse take him where it would.

In the distance a white tower rose above the treetops. "The Merlin

Tower!" exclaimed Prince Valiant, smiling for the first time since he had left King Arthur. For Val knew great affection for the wizard Merlin Ambrosius, advisor to the king. "Who else but Merlin can better help me escape the bewitchment of that hateful queen who chains me to her memory though she be at the other end of the world?" By this time Val had reached Merlin's abode and he entered forthwith.

For a full hour Val held forth about Aleta to Merlin, and the wizard remained silent. But finally he interrupted drily: "You wish contentment? To give up adventuring when and where it pleases you, and settle down to marriage and a family life?" "Well, no-o-o-o," replied Val. "I want adventure, a noble cause to fight for, good friends and splendid enemies. I want to travel far and wide, and . . . a maid to love."

"Poor, unhappy youth," murmured Merlin. "What else but this have you had all your life? As for contentment, that is a myth. Give a man all he wishes and he will be unhappy because he didn't wish for more. Only a turtle dozing on a sunny rock knows contentment. As for Aleta's magic you young idiot, what maid is not an enchantress? How else are young adventurers, willy-nilly, transformed into solid husbands? Now riddle me that!"

Merlin's sober common sense, leavened with affection and salted with good humor, had banished Aleta's spell. But as Val rode along it seemed to him he had lost something that he had become quite accustomed to. He felt no whit happier than before.

Memories . . . how many of them a man amassed, like coins in a strongbox, some tarnished, some shining bright. It was while he was in the fen, making his way to Horrit's hut, that the memories of his childhood came thronging back . . . the fishing . . . the hunting . . . his father. His father! Not in three crowded, adventuresome years had he seen his father.

Settled! He would visit him without delay.

Thereupon Val, acting on the impulse, returned at once to Camelot where he greeted his squire Beric and advised him to hold himself ready for a lengthy sea voyage. Then he craved King Arthur's leave to absent himself from Britain for awhile, which was granted. A few days later Val

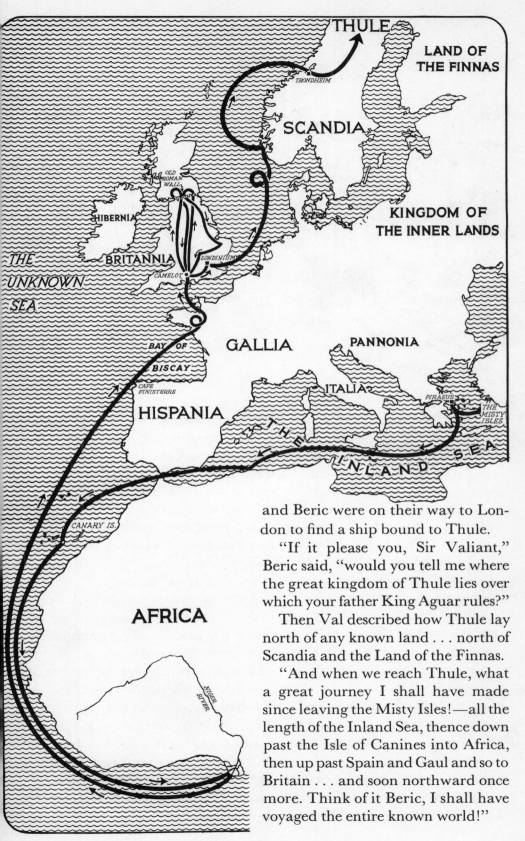

and Beric were on their way to London to find a ship bound to Thule.

"If it please you, Sir Valiant," Beric said, "would you tell me where the great kingdom of Thule lies over which your father King Aguar rules?"

Then Val described how Thule lay north of any known land . . . north of Scandia and the Land of the Finnas.

"And when we reach Thule, what a great journey I shall have made since leaving the Misty Isles!—all the length of the Inland Sea, thence down past the Isle of Canines into Africa, then up past Spain and Gaul and so to Britain . . . and soon northward once more. Think of it Beric, I shall have voyaged the entire known world!"

81

Reaching London, Val and his squire put up at a tavern and changed from the travel-stained garments they were wearing. They went to the water front in hopes of finding a ship northbound.

The narrow streets bounding the docks were remarkable for their fragrance . . . and it was not the fragrance of flowers.

There were ships from all parts of the world: sleek, swift Genoese and Venetian galleys with provision for two, three, four, and even more, ranks of rowers; fat trading vessels with mainmasts as tall as the ships were long.

One who was well versed in the shapes and sizes of hulls and sails and rig (as Val was not), and who could make sense of the maze of ropes and sheets and shrouds and yards and the manner of their manipulation (as Val could not), would have found much in the port of London whereat to be instructed and amused. For now that the world had become civilized, ships had grown great and strong and manageable, and could be depended upon to carry merchandise and news and learning everywhere; so that ships were as links in a vast chain that bound the nations together.

At last Val learned of a ship bound north to Scandia (Sweden). This was the Genoese merchantman *Poseidon,* and they went to see her at once. They found a crowd lining the quay, admiring her, for she was a new vessel, one of the largest yet built, with three towering masts, two sets of rowing ports, and two ornate "castles" fore and aft.

A boatman rowed Val and Beric out to the *Poseidon,* moored in mid-Thames. Presently they were in converse with her captain.

They found a crowd lining the quay, admiring the ship.

"Our destination is the city of Upsala in Scandia," he told them. "But first we will touch at Northland (Norway) where you can disembark and reach Thule by land." Finding the captain an agreeable man and his ship seaworthy, Val booked passage for himself and Beric. Promptly at dawn the

"But first we will touch at Northland (Norway) where you can disembark and reach Thule by land."

next morning they arrived on board. Val took note of his fellow-passengers who began arriving soon after. First came a venerable bearded merchant, Ahab of Tunis; then a second merchant, named Wattle, pompous and obviously wealthy. Next a blond young giant came vaulting over the rail cry-

84

ing: "I am Eric the Saxon, the greatest warrior alive!" The others were
Katwein Dravedatter and her mother Lady Olga, of Scandia; and Skurl,
Thane of Hedmark; and finally, though they were not passengers, a gang
of London convicts to man the oars. When all were aboard the captain
gave the word, the anchors were hoisted, the sails unfurled and the great

*The anchors were
hoisted, the sails
unfurled, and the
great ship dropped
down the Thames to
the open sea.*

And now the crew began making sport of the merchant Ahab.

The fun stopped suddenly, for it was unlucky to abuse the friend of a lusty knight.

ship dropped down the Thames on the ebb tide to the open sea. It was that same day that Val, lounging about the deck and enjoying the crisp sea air, noticed that most of the passengers were doing the same. He had already greeted the wealthy merchant Wattle and the loud-talking warrior Eric the Saxon when another passenger came on deck. This was the old man Ahab of Tunis. And now a curious and disquieting incident occurred. As Ahab approached, the merchant Wattle drew himself up pompously and said: "Stay away from me, usurer!" And now the crew, taking its signal from Wattle, began making sport of the old man, swilling his feet with bilge and playing other cruel tricks in which Wattle and Eric joined with considerable relish.

Val scowled. He did only one thing. He walked quietly up to Ahab and engaged him in friendly conversation. And the fun stopped suddenly, for it was held extremely unlucky to abuse the friend of a lusty young knight.

Val came closer to a real fight, however, in an incident that took place not long after. Katwein of Scandia was a comely maid and both Eric and Val took turns trying to charm her, Eric with tall tales of his battle prowess, Val with lute and song; but all either accomplished was to arouse the furious jealousy of Skurl, Thane of Hedmark, who (as all learned later) was insanely in love with the lass, though not she with him. The upshot was that Val and Skurl would have fought a duel to the death had not the captain himself intervened, threatening to throw both in chains.

But quarrels and duels were abruptly forgotten. For now the wind swung about, blowing up a squall. There was a great flapping of sails and creaking of gear. The sails were hurriedly furled; while below the convict oarsmen strained at the sweeps to keep the cumbersome craft from being

driven on the sands by the high wind and the heavy seas.

All night the struggle went on, passengers and crew working together; yet all to no avail, for there came a sickening crash, a pounding of the ship's bottom against the sand, and then . . . too strange for belief . . . a sudden calm as the ship seemed once more miraculously in deep water.

In the gray dawn light it was seen that the *Poseidon* had been washed over a sand bar and could not proceed on her journey until she was refloated over the bar into open water. This was done by transferring her cargo to small boats, then carrying the anchors seaward to the end of their cables, and with a full tide, windlassing the lightened ship inch by inch over the crest of the bar.

So again they were scudding up the North Sea with a sharp southwest wind in their sails. But though all seemed prosperous, none of the passengers knew that the *Poseidon's* timbers had been badly strained, and that she was now leaking dangerously.

It was perhaps two or three days later that Val detected a faint smoky haze and, prowling around, discovered a wisp of smoke issuing from a hatch. When the hatch was uncovered, smoke came billowing out. A shudder of horror passed through the ship. Fire!

While half the crew worked frantically at the *Poseidon's* pumps to keep her afloat, the rest poured water into her hold to quench the fire.

Yet truly the *Poseidon* was bedeviled by ill luck. For though the captain still hoped to overcome his double misfortune, it soon became obvious that a North Sea storm was making,

and would be upon them in full fury before another hour passed. And so indeed it was. The ship heeled over with the blow.

Clustered on the afterdeck the passengers watched the progress of the battle with tense emotions. To none among them was it a secret that their own lives depended on victory. And many despaired that this could be.

Vast quantities of water at length brought the fire under control; but not without its price. For the hold was well-nigh flooded, and under the lashing of the storm the seas grew monstrously big and ugly, so that they pounded still more leaks in the already staggering ship.

One last hope remained: to beach the *Poseidon* in some safe haven. By the captain's reckoning, the Northland coast could not be many miles to the northeast of their present position. But whether the ship could be made to stay afloat until some part of the Northland shore was reached was becoming every moment more doubtful.

And now, in these hours of greatest danger, captain and officers, passengers and crew all worked with the energy of desperation, turning the great wheeled pump till they sagged with exhaustion, then snatching a few minutes' rest and working again.

And deep down in the hold Val and many others hoisted buckets of water endlessly up to the weary arms above. But still the level of the water in the hold kept rising. For this was a battle against the mightiest of all foes . . . the Sea!

Slowly the *Poseidon* wallowed toward land; and as her hull sank lower

progress became ever slower until it scarce seemed as if she moved at all. Then the mist lifted and there, before them, was the blessed entrance to a calm Northland fjord. But alas for their joy. The ebb tide came roaring like a torrent through the narrow opening, catching the water-logged ship and swinging it crazily out of control. It struck full force against the rocks. The decks were awash. With difficulty the ship's boats were launched

while below deck the convict oarsmen were released that they might have a chance to swim to safety. In panic they surged on deck and crowded into the ship's boats, casting off with no heed to the safety of any but themselves. Those who remained on board, both passengers and crew, watched them go with the feeling that with them went the final chance of safety. For beneath their feet they could now feel the rending and tearing of timbers as the great ship tore itself apart. It was as though they were standing in their own sepulchers awaiting the direful moment when it would sink forever out of sight. Val was roused all at once by the whinnying of his charger who had been tied up in the stern of the

doomed ship. Val was starting toward the noble animal to set it free that it might with luck swim safely to shore when a spar, loosened by the storm, came crashing down. There was no time to get the charger out of the way . . . and Val shut his eyes in pain.

Val did what had to be done, quickly and mercifully. Then he stood and wept, for he had lost a friend.

Adversity and crisis often bring out the best in men's natures; but in some men they bring out what is most base. This was the case with the merchant Wattle and with Eric the Saxon. "The anger of the gods is upon us!" Val heard Eric bellowing as the confusion and panic on board worsened. "Yes, yes!" cried Wattle. "Ahab is hateful to them. Cast him into the sea and their anger will be appeased!" They might well have done this despicable deed, for they were already seizing Ahab, when Val strode over, sword drawn. The two men found this attitude very discouraging. Wattle scuttled off to gather his valuables, while Eric, after posing for a moment on the rail of the ship, plunged into the sea. It was noted that he tried to save none but himself.

All this time Skurl, who loved Katwein more than life itself, was trying with tragic intensity to find some means of getting her off the ship alive. But the maid—such was her perverse dislike of this lovelorn swain—refused even now in this frightful emergency to let him help her. Yet Skurl—such was his perverse love for this loveless maid—continued to try.

But the most tragic figure of all was the *Poseidon's* brave captain. He stood alone on the high stern-castle, looking with sadness at the havoc around him. No man loved the huge, unwieldy ship more than he. They would perish together.

Here the ship with a sudden lurch tilted over at such a sharp angle that most were thrown into the churning waves. The first to go, however unwillingly, was the fat merchant Wattle. Val caught sight of him sailing by, weighed down with several leathern pouches crammed with valuables. Val shouted: "You can't take it with you!" . . . but Wattle let nothing go.

The ship was breaking up with terrifying rapidity. The lofty mainmast cracked and fell. Skurl flung Katwein from its path and was himself caught under the wreckage. Then a great surge of water washed all overboard.

Val and Beric were swept ashore with Katwein. Lady Olga and Eric were safe. But certain it seemed that Skurl and Ahab were lost.

"Look! Two more survivors!" cried Beric. And there, amid the tossing wreckage, was Ahab clinging desperately to the unconscious Skurl. Val and Beric plunged into the thunderous surf and dragged them to safety.

And at that moment the little group on the beach saw the *Poseidon* sink below the surface of the water, with her brave captain going to the

bottom with her. Val now witnessed a scene which convinced him that under no circumstances would he ever thoroughly understand the ways of a woman. For now Katwein was kneeling over Skurl, trying her utmost to bring him back to life and sobbing: "I love you, Skurl . . . I love you." When Skurl opened his eyes again he was warm and comfortable and Katwein, with love shining in her blue eyes, was hovering over him. "So I died," he said, "and this is Heaven."

No, Val would never understand the ways of a woman.

Val now bade all the able-bodied survivors to gather what driftwood they could. Soon he had a cheerful fire blazing on the beach.

Then Eric the Saxon, sulky, because he had been ignored, vented his anger on Ahab, "Get back where you belong, merchant!"

"Eric, my over-loud friend," said Val with smiling lips and hard eyes, "this humble old man risked his life to rescue a helpless fellow-man. Make room for him at the fire, for you rescued nothing, not even your sword!"

Then Val rounded up some of the forlorn sailors, and with their help,

one of the ship's boats was salvaged. It was already badly battered but they set to work doing what they could to make it seaworthy once more.

By this time the fury of the storm had abated considerably. Val saw that the waters were thick with floating bales and boxes. The wrecked *Poseidon* itself could now be seen, as the tide ebbed, lying in fairly shallow water. Val now thought of a scheme whereby the group of survivors could come by food, clothing, and transportation, for he was certain that the native Northmen living in the nearby villages would soon discover the wreck and help themselves, unasked, to the rich cargo. He therefore sent a sailor in search of the nearest village with the following message: "A ship of immense size has been wrecked. Sir Valiant of King Arthur's Round Table bids you call your clan together and enrich yourselves with her cargo."

As Val had expected, the grateful Northmen for whom the salvage was an unexpected gift, gratefully offered the castaways all assistance. Lady Olga and Katwein were provided with horses while the injured Skurl was provided with a litter and guides to take them over the mountains to Hedmark. And so this party took its leave.

The rescued ship's boat was now in good repair again, and Val, having many miles still to go northward before reaching Thule, made ready to continue his journey with Beric. Ahab had business in Trondheim and begged leave to accompany Val, as did Eric. Finally the native Northmen helped them launch the boat through the tumbling surf and they were once more on their way. For Val this was beginning to be a real home-coming.

Summer skies and a sparkling sea! After the terrible hardships aboard the *Poseidon,* they felt like schoolboys on a holiday.

They followed along the jagged Northland coast, passing numberless fjords winding back through the high cliffs until they were lost in mysterious shadows. "I have often heard," Beric said, "that these same fjords are the abodes of goblins and elves and that witches hold their unholy sabbaths on the misty peaks."

They saw no sign of strange folk as day after day they sailed steadily northward, but saw only tidy villages shining white in the clear air. Often at dusk they beached their boat and sought food and other supplies at the nearest village. Always were they hospitably received and shown every simple kindness.

Thus at length they drew near Trondheim without knowing what a mighty disaster lay in store for them.

It was late one afternoon when suddenly there came a bump that shook their little craft from keel to masthead, as if the boat had dropped an arm's length.

100

"I know what this means," whispered Ahab in a voice filled with dread. "It is an earthquake deep under the sea and worse is to follow." Trembling, he pointed, "Look!"

Following his direction, they saw an ominous white line stretching across the horizon. Swifter than charging horsemen the tidal wave came roaring down upon them. The boat was flung upward like a twig

and, for a fearful instant, hung poised on the crest in a welter of spray. Then, as suddenly as it came, the mountainous wave passed under them. They found themselves rocking gently in a sea of hissing foam. But they were too dazed and shaken even to realize that the worst was over, that they were still alive.

Val was the first to recover. Quickly he lowered the sail. The boat was dangerously swamped, with its sides just barely above the surface. Then they all set to work, bailing frantically.

But at last the boat was cleared. Again the sail was hoisted. They hung out their sopping gear to dry in the sunshine and the fresh breeze. It was as if the earthquake and the tidal wave had been no more than some vaguely-remembered dream.

Thus they were spanking along when Eric remarked with no especial importance: "Just see what a strange cast there is to the water. It is the color of sepia."

Glancing at the sea around them Val and the rest all agreed that the cast of the water was indeed different from what it usually was, being of a curious blackness as if splotched with ink. "Probably mud stirred up from the bottom by the earthquake," said Val.

"The kraken!" gasped one of the sailors, suddenly horror-stricken. He pointed but Val was looking the other way. "The kraken," began Val, "is only an old Norse fable used to frighten—" But just then something writh-

"The kraken!" gasped one of the sailors.

ing and ghastly came coiling over the side of the boat. Val froze in sheer fright of this slimy, dripping arm. It remained for perhaps a minute, then slid over the side again.

Weirdly the water bubbled and frothed . . . then a huge gray mass floated sluggishly to the top of the black water. Two sinister eyes glared balefully as the boat glided by.

No one dared to move, for with a single sweep of its terrible arms the kraken could splinter the boat and carry them off to the bottom, there to feed on them. At any moment they expected the eyes to narrow in hate and the arms to lash out.

Perhaps it was too surfeited with food to interest itself in a boatload of human beings. At any rate and for whatever reason, it let the tiny craft drift by, close to its side, without molesting it.

Looking back they saw the kraken stirring. A second later it was thrashing the water to foam, lashing and writhing in a manner terrifying to behold. Val held his sword ready. Then all at once it sank below the black surface and was lost to sight.

"Well, that's that," said Val carelessly. "Not that there was really any danger . . ." But the hand that held the cup was shaking though he hoped no one had noticed.

In those brave days piracy was considered an honorable profession. Whenever the hardy Norsemen tired of tending their little farms, they took to their ships and went raiding. Friends and neighbors thought no less of them for that: indeed, friends and neighbors went along too. Val and his companions had been warned in advance of this Norse habit, and cautioned against sailing by night lest they fall prey to the sea robbers. They therefore spent each night ashore and sailed only by day. But before they could reach Trondheim, which was now only a few days' journey north, a pirate found them. It happened in this wise.

It was near dusk and they were veering toward the rocky shore when they saw that a sail was bearing down on them in a manner too menacing to admit of any mistake as to its intentions. "On guard!" said Val. And here Eric the Saxon, who had been mopping the bilge from the deck, turned a trick of surprising slyness. Before the pirate came too near he slapped the dirty rag sharply in front of Ahab's face. Then, when the pirate drew up alongside, its men prepared to board and plunder, Eric shouted across the water: "We have but one thing of value aboard . . . a wealthy merchant whom we are holding for ransom—if he lives that long, for he is very sick."

And now the Norsemen saw Ahab's pale face all covered with hideous red spots. "He has the pox! Sail on!" cried the pirate captain. Later the "pox" was cured by a simple wash, and all laughed gaily . . . except the

*Before the pirate came too near
Eric slapped the dirty rag
sharply in front of Ahab's face.*

pirates. And so they reached Trondheim and were puzzled to see such a vast gathering of ships and richly dressed nobles. In gratitude Ahab now

gave Val a satin doublet lined with mail for his safety; then Val set out to
learn the meaning of all the activity in town. From some retainers he soon

Val carefully covered over the hilt and scabbard of the Singing Sword.

discovered that King Valgrind of the Inner Lands was on his way to sign a treaty with Aguar, King of Thule. In celebration of the event there was to be a week of feasting and games.

The news elated Val. To his companions he announced: "My father, the King of Thule, will hold a tournament. Disguised as a humble troubadour, I'll win the prize, and then reveal myself as his long-absent son." (Hearty young lads of this age were

Then Val was roughly thrust aside by a courtier to make way for the king.

But for Beric, Val might have involved himself in a quarrel with Valgrind.

usually that overconfident!) So Val carefully covered over the gleaming hilt and jewelled scabbard of the Singing Sword and set out on the last leg of his long journey. His faithful squire Beric and Eric the Saxon walked at the side of Val's donkey. Val no longer looked the knight. Instead, with his lute and his plain garb he passed for what he pretended to be: a wandering musician. He wondered what sort of man this King Valgrind might be. It was not long before he discovered, and in a most unpleasant manner.

For it is related that Val and his companions were proceeding along a narrow trail when suddenly a troop of mounted courtiers came riding up with King Valgrind in their midst. Then Val was roughly thrust aside to make way for the king. Quick to resent this violence, Val's hand flew to his sword-hilt. And but for Beric, who cautioned him to restraint, Val might

rashly have involved himself in a serious quarrel with Valgrind and his nobles and so have upset his father's careful statecraft. With his two friends he stood aside as the courtiers rode by.

"So that's King Valgrind," Val muttered, staring at the hard, haughty face with the shrewd eyes.

They followed the king's party and about mid-afternoon descended into a wooded valley. Here the king's party stopped to await the arrival of their baggage train which was coming after them at a slow pace.

Val got a sudden idea. He ordered camp set up in a secluded spot and settled down to watch the trail. Presently the king's baggage train started passing. For a long time it went by. Finally Val said: "I see sure signs of treachery. Mark this—no ladies have been taken along; there are more soldiers than are necessary for a peaceful celebration and, lastly, the great number of servants are broad-shouldered and clumsy at their unaccustomed tasks. They are warriors in disguise!"

Val now purposed to spy out Valgrind's moves. To this end he went to the king's camp with Eric. "I am a troubadour and juggler," he said, "and this is Eric, a most stalwart fighter. We both wish to join the ranks of good King Valgrind's followers." The master-at-arms was glad to engage so brawny a warrior as Eric; and Val was hired to amuse king and courtiers

Presently the king's
baggage train started
passing. For a long
time it went by.

113

with his ballads and his sly tricks
learned long years ago from Slith. At
last he won Valgrind's attention and
for reward was tossed a few pennies;
but the real reward was the freedom
with which he was allowed to roam
the camp. He kept his ears open, and
begged Eric to do the same. Listening
was a real hardship for Eric, who all
his life had favored talking; but he
did it. It was Val, however, who over-
heard one noble remarking to another
as they looked over a beautiful stretch
of rolling meadow in which Val's
father's herds were grazing: "I hope
this smiling estate falls to my share!"

Could there any longer be doubt as
to Valgrind's evil designs?

Then came the day when Val stood
gazing down upon the scene of his
childhood . . . the great stone castle of
Vikingsholm which even now a
treacherous king was preparing to
seize by guile and trickery. He wondered if he could prevent this doom.

For a long moment he stood, then

turned and joined King Valgrind's all too numerous soldiers, and entered the great courtyard he remembered so well. He took good care to appear to be a stranger; yet he was almost betrayed, and most unexpectedly, when an old man, seeing him, uttered a cry of joy and knelt in homage. "Welcome home, my prince!" Val jerked him to his feet, cautioning: " 'Tis you,

Erland replied: "Most of them have been called to our borders to quell the Finnas' raids."

Erland, my old teacher! Greetings! ... But keep my name secret!" Then he went with the old man to a quiet place and asked: "Why are there so few of my father's soldiers about?"

To this Erland replied with troubled mien: "Most of them have just been called to our eastern borders to quell the Finnas' raids. The Finnas are allies of King Valgrind."

And later, from Eric the Saxon, came yet worse news. "Valgrind's men are under orders to stand by their arms, ready for action ..."

Val trusted Eric, believing him boastful but loyal. In this he was mistaken. For Eric thought to himself: "King Valgrind will reward me if his plans succeed. On the other hand

Prince Valiant has thwarted me all too often. I owe him nothing."

But of these treacherous thoughts Val was unaware as on the castle balustrade he sang love ballads in a clear young voice. The maids of Thule who listened to this ragged troubadour with the impudent, bold look in his dark eyes . . . who were intrigued by his reckless, devil-may-care manner, had not the slightest notion that they were being entertained by the prince of the realm—by King Aguar's own son. But how could they know when the king himself did not?

Indeed King Aguar—for at this sunset hour he had put aside the cares of state and was standing and listening alone on his balcony—looked down and murmured: "Not since my son left have I heard so merry a voice." He looked down again, then continued: "Just another minstrel, but a well set-up young rascal. My wandering son would be about that age now. And he, too, would be beguiling my young guests with idiotic nonsense if he were here. . . . If . . . he . . . were . . . here . . ." repeated the king, staring hard. And suddenly his heart sang. "Oh my glorious, good-for-nothing, splendid son! Oh Val, you high-hearted young fool . . . play your game out!

"Valgrind just now conferred with his knights. . . . Whatever treachery is planned will take place tonight."

I'll not give your secret away till you come to me and cry, *Father!*"

But in another part of the castle King Valgrind was playing a more deadly game. Old Erland came secretly to Val to report that the final touches were being put on the plot that would pluck the kingdom of Thule like a ripe plum. "Valgrind just now conferred with his knights . . . they are ordered to make no preparations for tomorrow's tournament. So whatever treachery is planned will take place at the banquet tonight."

And old Erland was apparently correct in surmising that the final stroke in Valgrind's plot was timed to take place during the course of the banquet; for, later that evening, Val noticed how Valgrind's nobles streamed into the great hall heavily armed. To add to Val's anxiety, he was obliged to wait in the corridor. Every moment he expected to hear a scream and know thereby that his father was being assassinated. But for the time being he was spared this awful event. All he heard were voices and laughter and the gay clatter of bowls and cups. Suddenly one of the warrior-guards stationed inside the great hall came to the door. "Bestir yourself, troubadour—King Valgrind desires you to enter and sing for the noble company while they sup. Make haste . . ."

But no song of romance did Val sing. Instead he roared forth the old war chants of ancient Thule. And the warriors of Thule seated at the feast beat out the time with their fists and felt the hot lust for battle surge into their hearts.

Even while he was singing Val saw Valgrind's soldiers slowly edging in at every door, then waiting for a signal. The hour of basest treachery was at hand.

The last song was sung. Val slipped away. He quickly armed. To Beric and old Erland he said: "Do what I have told you to do without fail!" Then he descended the secret stairway that came up behind the throne.

Haughty Valgrind felt an arm of steel around his neck. There was no time to make an outcry. Suddenly his chair was empty. His departure was so swift and silent that it was a full minute before he was missed by his fol-

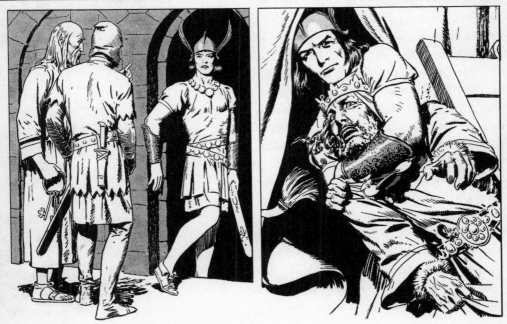

121

lowers. But some held later that King Aguar of Thule appeared somewhat less surprised than he should have been at this abrupt withdrawal of his guest of honor.

King Valgrind made queer guttural noises in his throat as he was dragged through the dark passage behind the throne, then up a narrow stone stairway. He had no idea where he was being taken nor by whom.

Meanwhile in the great hall there was consternation. The men of the Inner Lands began dimly to understand that their plot had somehow become undone, for it was no part of the arrangement for Valgrind to vanish. They looked about, undecided whether to fall on the Thule warriors at once or to hold their tempers until they learned the whereabouts of their missing king.

King Aguar had already motioned his guards. They stood ready.

At that moment, on a small balcony high above the heads of all, appeared Sir Valiant, Knight of the Round Table, heir to the throne of Thule. In one fist was King Valgrind, in the other his naked, gleaming sword.

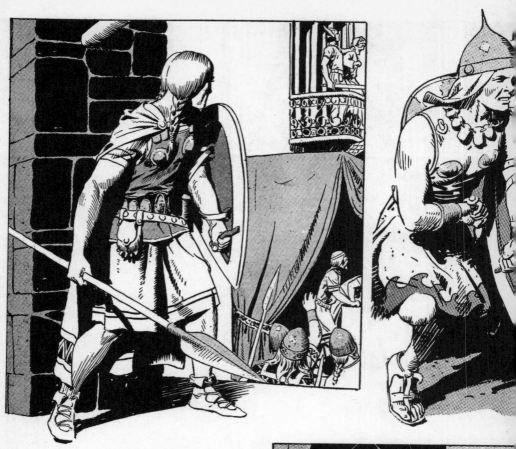

"Men of the Inner Lands!" he called
down. "Sit still or you'll be without a
king!"

Then Eric the Saxon had another
change of heart. His instructions
from Val had been to alert King
Aguar's palace garrison as soon as
Valgrind and his men rose up. Only
Eric had not thought it possible for
Valgrind's well-laid treachery to mis-
carry. He had therefore intended to
do nothing and thereby earn the
gratitude of the ruler of the Inner
Lands. Perhaps he might even be
made a nobleman and share in the
partition of Thule.

"By Thor and Odin," said Eric as
in admiration he watched Valiant
single-handedly deprive the vicious
Inner Lands' nobles of their leader,

"a lad who can do the likes of this is a leader worth following!"

With that, Eric fetched the garrison on the run.

The Thule soldiers closed and barred all the doors leading from the great hall, allowing no one to enter or to leave.

For a moment after Valiant had shouted down from the balcony, the treacherous nobles had looked as if they might defy him even though it meant the death of their king. But when the doors were slammed shut and they saw that the galleries above were lined with grim-faced archers with taut bowstrings and arrows pointed at their hearts, they slumped uneasily in their seats.

For them the battle was over . . . and lost. But they still had hopes that King Valgrind would somehow manage to talk himself out of his

125

peril and so save them all. Even now they could see their king pleading with the young prince.

It is perhaps fortunate that the nobles of the Inner Lands could not hear what their king was saying to Val in his frantic effort to save his own skin.

"I give you my permission, Sir Valiant, to hang as many of my nobles as it may please you and your royal sire, the thrice-honored ruler of Great Thule. For it was these same nobles, and not I, who urged on me this treachery against your nation."

Val gazed ahead in stony silence.

"Come, Sir Valiant," urged the desperate king, "is it money you wish? I will give you a fortune. Is it lands? I will give you more acres than your eyes can see riding from sunrise to sunset on a galloping charger. Do you wish castles? I will give you mine, and more. I will give you my only daughter, the princess, in marriage so that at my death you may rule with her as king of the rich Inner Lands."

And this time Prince Valiant spoke, saying: "Those who come in the name of peace and friendship to steal and kill are far worse than open enemies. For it is better to fall in battle against a splendid foe than to die of a knife in the back dealt by the hand of false friendship."

Then King Valgrind knew he was doomed and the blood left his face and he seemed suddenly to have grown old and ready for the grave.

It was then that King Aguar ascended the hidden stairway, accompanied by his guards. Without a word, Prince Valiant turned the trembling king over to his father.

King Valgrind made one final, pitiful plea. Taking off his crown, he held it forth to King Aguar. "Cousin," he cried, "all that I own is yours to have and to hold forever. Only spare me my life . . ."

King Aguar did not so much as glance at Valgrind. He merely motioned with his hand. The golden crown clattered to the floor as the guards seized him. There was one sharp scream. Beyond this, nothing more was ever heard of King Valgrind, save only the tale that a king had once come to sign a treaty of peace and had stayed to find peace everlasting.

With the going of King Valgrind, father and son, king and prince, nodded to each other there in the half-lit corridor outside the balcony.

"Good evening, Father," said Val courteously, "I trust you have been well?" . . . "Tolerably, son," answered the king in a friendly voice. "Will you be staying to supper?"

King Aguar did not glance at Valgrind. He merely motioned.

There came then a long moment of silence. At last Val observed: "My father is a crybaby." —"And the last time my son shed a tear," the king reminded him, "the palm of my hand was stinging."

Next morning, the apprehensive prisoners in the banquet hall were interviewed. King Aguar told them: "Your homeland is now undefended and we could easily conquer it. But we don't want it. We give you all your freedom . . . upon payment of a suitable ransom, of course." And so it was that the nobles of the Inner Lands returned homeward one by one.

And now King Aguar threw off all the anxiety and loneliness of the past three years and, with Val at his side, there was much gaiety throughout Thule. But even as laughter ran all about him, deep within Valiant's heart, a memory still remained . . . a maid with golden hair from a far-off isle, who likewise laughed, mocking, challenging, daring him to come back.

5521   The End